Contemporary Chinese Poetry
in English Translation Series

Luo Fu
Selected Poems

Translated by
Leon Burnett, Xu Xiaofan and others

教育部人文社会科学重点研究基地
安徽师范大学中国诗学研究中心 组编
Chinese Poetry Research Center of Anhui Normal University

杨四平 主编　　上海文化出版社

当代汉诗英译丛书

洛夫诗歌英译选

CONTENTS

目录

THE POMEGRANATE TREE

If your promise was carved into the
    pomegranate tree
the fruit would hang heavier from its branches.

Face up, I lie beneath the tree; face up, the stars lie
    among its leaves.
Every tree belongs to me; I exist in each of them.
While they exist, love will never desert me.

Tenderly the pomegranates ripen.
Each one, bursting
sparkles, sparkles with your name.

石榴树

假若把你的诺言刻在石榴树上
枝桠上悬垂着的就显得更沉重了

我仰卧在树下，星子仰卧在叶丛中
每一株树属于我，我在每一株树中
它们存在，爱便不会把我遗弃

哦！石榴已成熟，这动人的炸裂
每一颗都闪烁着光，闪烁着你的名字

WINTER'S DIARY

Last spring, I chopped down a willow tree outside the house.

Its creaking got on my nerves. I cut it up

and tossed the pieces into the stove.

The old leaf-sweeper next door speaks ill of me behind my back.

The melodious birds rebuke me, knocking their beaks against

    my window,

and the poet complains, too:

    Without the willow branches

    Where will the moon rest?

(All this noted down for the 13th in my diary.)

Winter has come early this year. In the night

some travellers from the south arrived in the snowstorm,

so I secretly thrust my diary into the stove

for the one who sits by the fire to resent himself.

冬天的日记

春天，嫌阶前的一棵柳树太吵
我把它砍下，劈成一小块一小块
投进了炉子

隔壁的扫叶老人背着我说许多坏话
鸟雀们谱成曲子骂我，啄我的窗
而诗人也在埋怨：
　　没有那些柳枝
　　月亮往哪里挂？
（这些，我都记在日记本的十三号里）

今年冬天来得早，昨夜
风雪中有一队旅人从南方来了
于是，我偷偷把日记本塞进了炉子
让烤火的人去恨自己

WHEN THE GRAPES RIPEN

They wait a long time for a hand to crush them

The liquid, blushing face streams through me
like a sweet memory, and a vessel, unadorned,
Brews a seasonal malady, a kind of melancholy
    The melancholy — it may be beautiful
    it may have been gleaned by a child from beyond the wall

If the promise of Dionysus can fill
so ample a cup
drunkenness is no different from innocence
or rather it's a form of completion

My mind is constant, like the mellow juice contained
within the grape's skin
all that is solitary and forbearing must be at peace
—Love is patient

葡萄成熟时

久久等候一只手的捏破

流质，羞红的脸，如甜美的时光
倾注于我的，没有雕饰的容器
酿制着某一种季节病，某一种忧郁
　　　那忧郁——也许很美
　　　也许是一个孩子从墙外拾来

如果获奥尼赛斯的诺言能盛满
这么大的一只杯
醉是一种纯真
一个完成

我的神智常在，如醇美的葡萄汁被表皮包着
凡是孤独的，凡是宽容的，都必如此宁静
　　——爱是恒久忍耐

ON THIS ISLAND

Mystical trees that have leaves like green eyes and
    no names grow on this island
Their tentacle roots reach deep into the rocks to
    explore the secrets of time
On my knees, I scoop and drink from life's
    running spring
that lurks and gurgles in the woods, the way the heart
    takes in its blood
When the lithe wings of a bird kiss the sinking star
I shall embrace the rising sun and the sails returning
    to this island

When I learned that dead leaves seek burial to make
    the earth fertile
I no longer wept at midnight or scoured the beach for
    the faint hues of the setting sun
or played on the flute, since sorrow no longer lodged
    in my eyes
Indoors, in the dark, I smashed the palette used for
    making self-portraits
and packed my bag, silently counting the grains of
    dust on my travelling clothes
as a seed will carefully count the days before
    sending forth its buds

这岛上

这岛上，有神奇的无名树与绿眼睛的叶
根须的触角伸向岩石里，探索时间的奥义
林间隐伏着也激响着的是生命的流泉
我会匍地掬饮，亦如心脏之吸取血液
当飞鸟轻快的翅膀吻着那将沉落的星辰
在岛上，我将迎接朝阳，迎接海上的归帆

当我知道落叶祈求埋葬是为了土地的富饶
我再不在午夜啜泣，在海滩上寻觅淡淡的残阳
再不吹弄那支笛，因悲伤已不在我眼里栖息
摔碎那块在暗室专为自己画像的调色板
检点行囊，默默数着征衣上的砂粒
如种子在地层下细数着出土的日期

THE SONG OF TOM

Tom, the twenty-year-old man, is made at last
into a bronze statue in the plaza
his name chiselled
on the wind

Time to wipe the gun clean
time to smoke the pipe
time to think of time no longer
(to draw a naked woman on the ground with
a bayonet
and cut her in half at the waist)
to scoop and drink from one's own image in the river
when there is no wine
and to breathe from one's wounds
when there is no mouth

After dying a thousand deaths
he finally made his way into the plaza
holding his head up high

汤姆之歌

二十岁的汉子汤姆终于被人塑成
一座铜像在广场上
他的名字被人刻成
一阵风

擦枪此其时
抽烟此其时
不想什么此其时
(用刺刀在地上画一个裸女
然后又横腰把她切断)
没有酒的时候
到河边去捧饮自己的影子
没有嘴的时候
用伤口呼吸

死过千百次
只有这一次他才是仰着脸
进入广场

A HEAVY MIND

That old shirt of mine

hangs on the wall

from a mail

pending judgement

My hair is dyed

my dentures have serial numbers

my wounds

issue blood, not words

I used to be conversant with the Five Classics and

the Six arts

I used to behave well and keep my hair short

I would settle my accounts in good time

Why is my old shirt

left hanging

on the wall?

心事

我的那件旧衬衣
未经审判
就那么吊在墙壁的
钉子上

我的头发是染过的
我的假牙是编过号的
我的伤口
除了流血之外甚么也没说
我曾熟读五经六艺
行事规矩不留长发
按期缴纳房租，报费，分期付款等等
干吗仍把我的
那件旧衬衣
吊死在
墙上

MOON SINKING, ON THE ROOF

From the roof on the fourth floor

the moon

sinks in three or five abstruse postures

It makes one wonder why

so much dust floats in the daylight

Yet what weighs more heavily than the

autumnal chill

are the clothes that never dried in the sun

and the dripping tap

from next door

屋顶上的落月

四楼屋顶上
月亮
以三五种晦涩的姿式下沉
白昼为什么那么多浮尘
令人苦思不解

而，比秋寒更重的
是未曾晒干的衣服
是隔壁
自来水龙头的
漏滴

THE STORY OF THE STONE

So

you are after all a stone

Silence grows from inside

after your bones become too brittle to utter a sound

So

you lie down by the road

unclad, slow-witted:

waiting quietly

until the saliva on your face

is dried in the wind

石头记

所以说
你毕竟是一块石头
静寂自内部生长
自你的骨骼硬得无声之后

所以说
你痴呆地
脱光衣服躺在路旁
静待着
脸上的唾沫
风干

AGITATION OF A SNAKE

How could a cold heart make
the blood in its veins boil?
A good question
Stiffening its old skin, it broods
and brews a cold grudge
squeezing it through venomous teeth

At times it coils up for the winter
hatching a small egg
of the sun
At times it sways and rises
to the tune of the charmer
until its body resembles
a rose

蛇之骚动

冰凉的意念
又如何能使脉管中的血水飞腾？
说的也是
它抱自己的蜕衣沉思
它把冷却后的悲忿
从一口毒牙中
逼出

有时就这么盘蜷过冬
孵一枚小小的
太阳之卵
另些时候则沿着弄蛇者的笛音
爬升
及至舞成
一朵蔷薇

THE SQUARE

What are you

when you are the centre of the storm?

I am closest to the sun

at noon, when no shadow falls

and I occupy the centre

Redundant an explanation

of how beads of sweat fertilise history

On this square

the doves peck away half of my afternoon

the other half wasted

in exchanging gazes with the bronze statue

I wait for the gun to fire

but what then, when it does?

Bugles sound at the lowering of the flag

reminding me, over and over again, of tomorrow's glory

Clatter of boots dying away:

how can you pretend not to understand!

广场

什么塑造了你
当你塑造了暴风雨的中心
正午，我往往站在中央
往往使自己觉得距太阳最近
影子自无必要
说汗水将如何如何肥沃一部历史
亦无必要
广场上
鸽子啄去了我半个下午
另一半浪费在
与铜像深深的对视上
我在等待炮声
而炮声响起时又将如何
降旗的号音
一再强调我们明日的辉煌
咯咯而去的靴子啊
你岂可装作不懂

MUSINGS IN MARCH

The anxious mind

empties itself into the brimming ashtray

Looking up at the ceiling

I sculpt the jade of your face with cigarette smoke

Snow comes into my mind

The moon-coloured blouse at the bottom of the chest

comes into my mind

You said its touch makes you cold

yet when I tug at your sleeve, ever so gingerly

my hand burns

Not because of fire, to be sure

Holding you by the hand

I feel a March full of snowstorms

in your palm

三月之惑

烟缸中
堆满了化灰的心事
仰望天花板
把你的脸琢成
一块烟雾氤氲的玉
我突然想到雪

想到箱子底下那件月白的衫子
你说越穿越冷
我轻轻拉你的衣角时
却又烫手
无论如何决不是火

握你时
你掌中仍是
大雪纷飞的三月

WATER AND FIRE

I wrote down four lines about water

and drank three of them

The surviving line

became an icicle in your body

I wrote down five lines about fire

two for brewing the tea

two for warmth in winter

The surviving line

is for you to read to me in the evenings when the

lights go out

水与火

写了四行关于水的诗
我一口气喝掉三行
另外一行
在你体内结成了冰柱

写了五行关于火的诗
两行烧茶
两行留到冬天取暖
剩下的一行
送给你在停电的晚上读我

THE WORK OF THE WIND

I rambled along the river

yesterday

to where the reeds bend to drink

I asked the chimney

to write a long, long letter in the sky

It writes only in longhand

My mind is bright

like the candlelight in your window

Forgive me

for the occasional smudge

It's the work of the wind

It doesn't matter

whether the letter makes sense

What matters

is that you take the time

before all the daisies wither

to be angry

or amused

to find my flimsy shirt in the chest

and to brush your soft, black hair

then to light a lamp

with the love of a lifetime

I am the fire

that can die down any minute

It's the work of the wind

因为风的缘故

昨日我沿着河岸
漫步到
芦苇弯腰喝水的地方
顺便请烟囱
在天空为我写一封长长的信
潦是潦草了些
而我的心意
则明亮亦如你窗前的烛光
稍有暧昧之处
势所难免
因为风的缘故

此信你能否看懂并不重要
重要的是
你务必在雏菊尚未全部凋零之前
赶快发怒，或者发笑
赶快从箱子里找出我那件薄衫子
赶快对镜梳你那又黑又柔的妩媚
然后以整生的爱
点燃一盏灯
我是火
随时可能熄灭
因为风的缘故

THE WATER LILIES

The water lilies in the pond beside the Nagasaki
atom bomb memorial have kept witness for decades...

Upon the surface of the water

the dust falls

The sonic boom kills with a thousand decibels

Across the distance

two atom bombs glare at each other

Enclosed by ripples

the water lilies turn aside

once more

with a heavy heart

Below the surface of the water

— the mud, the abyss, the cell

where purgatorial fires burn

and a million drops of blood condense into

black fossils

May 10, 1987

睡莲

长崎原子弹纪念碑旁的一池睡莲数十年来未曾合眼……

水之上
是扬尘
是音爆，千个分贝的杀伤力
是万里以外
两颗核子飞弹的怒目而视
水中央，风叠层浪
睡莲拥着一池月光的心事
又翻了一次身

水之下
是污泥
是沉渊，炼火的囚室
是天地之间
千万滴被熬成黑色化石的血

一九八七·五·十

MORNING BELLS IN A MOUNTAIN TEMPLE

Dense fog in the mountains

opens a vast void between earth and sky

The temple has barely finished its desolate dream

before the dawn bells confront it

with their sumptuous, inky splash

They strike the mountain peak opposite

with a clang, and the echo

is mixed with a cry of labour pains

below the horizon

before the birth of the sun

July 12, 1988

山寺晨钟

满山浓雾
为天地布下一大片空白
山寺
刚做完一场荒凉的梦
晨钟便以泼墨的方式
一路洒了过去
哐地一声撞在对面山顶上
回声中夹杂着
地平线下太阳分娩时
阵痛的叫喊

一九八八·七·一二

THE DEATH OF AUTUMN

Among things most unbearable
are nearby snores before sunset:
verbose, trivial snores
So I go to the mountains, crutch in hand
clasping a key in my right-hand pocket
warm in the sharp autumnal air

The poking crutch encounters
the lifeless moulting of a cicada
Autumn dies ever so gradually:
that is where its beauty lies

秋之死

日落前
最不能忍受身边有人打鼾
唠唠叨叨，言不及义
便策杖登山
天凉了，右手紧紧握住
口袋里一把微温的钥匙

手杖一阵拨弄
终于找到一枚惨白的蝉蜕
秋，美就美在
淡淡的死

A LETTER

I received a letter yesterday

containing a pinch of ash

Brushing away the ash, I saw a face:

yours, as expected. You know

only too well

how I cherish the cinders of tenderness

and all that is sealed within the rock

信

昨天收到一封信
打开信封发现只有一撮灰
拨开灰烬看到一张脸
果然是你，只有你
深知我很喜欢焚过的温柔
以及锁在石头里的东西

FUNERAL RITES FOR A POEM

A love poem, shut away

for thirty years in a drawer

is cast into the fire

Words

crackle in the flames

but the ash remains silent

It believes

the poem will finally be read

by someone

in the wind

诗的葬礼

把一首
在抽屉里锁了三十年的情诗
投入火中

字
被烧得吱吱大叫
灰烬一言不发
它相信
总有一天
那人将在风中读到

A PAPER CUT-OUT OF A FACE

If my face

is cut into a landscape drained of blood

then woe to the world

Here is my pale forehead,

mistaken for the ruins of history

My eyebrows:

two fatalistic leaves fallen

Small galaxies

appear on the black paper

Peeping out from my pupil

the moon tumbles down my cheek

like a teardrop

It doesn't require scissors of tempered steel

but a deft, measured hand instead

One stroke

and the pieces of hair and skin fall

Further trimmings darken the face (the pain is only

secondary)

made all the more impenetrable

by the sustained gaze

May, 1994

纸剪的脸

把我的脸
剪成一幅失血的风景
悔憾是属于全世界的
这明明是我那苍白的额
偏有人说是历史的废墟
而眉毛
则是
两片宿命的落叶
黑色的纸上
出现几个小小的星空
从眼瞳的部位望出去
月亮，一滴泪似的
向颊边滚落

剪刀不必是纯钢打制
手法则须细致而具韵律感
一刀下去
毛发皮肤纷纷而落
脸，越修越黑
痛还在其次，只是
越看
越像一部晦涩的
玄学

一九九四·五

DECONSTRUCTION

Life is an extravagant gown, riddled with lice.

- Eileen Chang

Yesterday

putting on this extravagant gown by chance

I discarded yesterday, and kept the gown

Today

forced into this extravagant gown

I discard today, and keep the gown

Tomorrow

putting on this extravagant gown again by accident

I shall discard tomorrow, and keep the gown

To keep the gown

is to keep the lice

To keep the lice

is to keep the past

and the itch

March, 1996

解构

生命是一袭华美的袍，爬满了虱子
　　　　　　　　——张爱玲

昨日
我偶然穿上这一袭华美的袍
我脱去昨日，留下了袍

今日
我被迫穿上这一袭华美的袍
我脱去今日，留下了袍

明日
我无意中又穿上这一袭华美的袍
我脱去明日，留下了袍

留下了袍子
便留下了虱子
留下了虱子
便留下了历史和
痒

　　　　　　　　一九九六·三

THE SILENT PUMPKIN

The tendrils roll in
from a realm that is not human.
The longer the vines of the pumpkin grow
the shorter my lines
become

The pumpkin is silent because
there is nothing left to say
Its belly swells
splits
spilling sweetness
with a whiff of devilwood
stale from last night
and utterly unintelligible

October, 1996

南瓜无言

藤蔓，从无人处
汹涌而来
南瓜藤越长越长
我的诗
越写越短

南瓜无言
正因为无话可说
肚皮越长越大
剖开
一半很甜
另一半带点隔夜的木樨花味
不知所云

一九九六·十

CHANCE DISCOVERIES IN THE BACKYARD

I caught sight of a raccoon yesterday
Our mutual gaze lasted long
An ephemeral sense of eternity flashed on me

With only one bony hand
the trees hold many bodies, once fleshy, once tender
Let me not rot away entirely
so that my bones and sinews, dried in the air
may still clutch the dead twigs

Let the words that have a husk but no core
and the silences that have a core but no husk
and the hair and the skin
fly away in the wind

October, 1996

后院偶见

昨天，甚至看到一只浣熊
我和它对视良久
有种永恒之感
一闪而逝

树们只用一只瘦瘦的手
悬吊着
那么多曾经丰腴过的肉身
我希望自己不再溃烂
让风干的一点筋骨
继续黏在枯枝上

至于那些有壳无核的话语
有核无壳的沉默
以及毛发皮肤等等
就任它随风而去吧

一九九六·十

A BURIAL

Before the heavy snow covered the earth

he spent the whole morning

meditating on the inner logic of things

First he swept the fallen leaves

and then he dug the earth

to give the frozen squirrel its funeral

Then he cremated

his old padded coat riddled with neo-classical lice

and buried the ashes

which still smouldered

April, 1997

埋

大雪降落之前
整个上午
他在思索事物本身的逻辑
先扫落叶
继而挖土
为一只冻死的松鼠料理后事
继而火焚
那件爬满了新古典主义虱子的旧棉袄
继而埋下
仍在蠕蠕而动的
一堆灰

一九九七·四

IN THE WINDOW, WITH WIND AND RAIN OUTSIDE

Wind and rain do not bear close scrutiny

In the window
stands a bowl of pink daffodils
The flowers start to rinse
their pink faces

Then they doze off
Their heads
rested
against a March that is neither wet nor dry

风雨窗前

风雨是不能细究的东西

窗前
一盆水仙
开始把粉脸
一层层
剥下来洗

然后就打起瞌睡来
头
搁在
心情不湿，也不干的
三月里

FROM WHERE THE RAIN COMES

From the mountains

from beyond the window

from the eaves

from among the chattering lotuses

from within the rocks

where the crickets sing their lonesome songs

But no!

It comes from your cold

icy Interrogations

雨从何处来

从山上
从窗外
从屋檐
从众荷的鼓噪中来
从石头内部
蛐蛐的寂寞的鸣叫中来

不
从你这冷冷的
问话中来

A FLY

An erratic fly

inspects the room

settling on the wall clock

over its chosen digit

Time moves forward:

the fly stays still

outside time

elusively

I tiptoe to follow. It's off again

resting on the whitewashed wall

It nubs its hands. It rubs its feet

Its vigilant, dark-blue compound eyes

scrutinise my unreal existence with contempt

I keep approaching quietly, with a raised hand

It rubs its hands. It rubs its feet

It must be craving afternoon tea

its breath

fine-tuned to the cosmos

It nubs its hands. It rubs...

Zap! Goes my forceful strike

yet it's off, all the same

It escapes my fingers

buzzbuzzing

In its stead

my shattered, blood-stained shadow

collapses instantly down the wall

苍蝇

一只苍蝇
绕室乱飞
偶尔停在壁钟的某个数字上
时间在走
它不走
它是时间以外的东西
最难抓住的东西
我蹑足追去，它又飞了
栖息在一面白色的粉墙上
搓搓手，搓搓脚
警戒的复眼，近乎深蓝
睥睨我这虚幻的存在
扬起掌
我悄悄向它逼近
搓搓手，搓搓脚
它肯定渴望一杯下午茶
它的呼吸
深深牵引着宇宙的呼吸
搓搓手，搓……
我冷不防猛力拍了下去
嗡的一声
又从指缝间飞走了

而，墙上我那碎裂沾血的影子
急速滑落

A CARPET OF SNOW

Words of snow are not cold

but quiet

Crows caw from the rooftop: they scare

the old dog next door, and silence it for the night

The crows flock in December

They speak

with their black bodies

and austere looks

Their open mouths

retch forth

the cold moonlight that covers the earth

雪地

雪说的话并不冷
只是没有声音
屋顶上乌鸦的啼叫
吓得隔壁的老狗安静了一夜

鸦，从十二月飞来
以全身的黑，以及
寡欲的眼神
说话
一张嘴
哇
吐了满地冰凉的月光

NO ANSWER IN THE END

He is used to writing letters on the beach
Some words are carried away by the sunset
Some are washed away by the tide
The hermit crab passes by
adding a couple of lines
post-haste

An empty can
sings for an entire afternoon, all by itself
Spanning the vast expanse between heaven and earth
is the water: does it have a family name?
The sea falls and rises
but gives no answer in the end
before falling again

终归无答

他习惯在沙滩上写信
有些话被夕阳带走
有些话被潮水冲走
寄居蟹路过时
又草草地
添了两句

一只空罐头
独自唱了一下午
天地悠悠
水姓什么？
海，沉下去
终归无答
它再次沉了下去

THE MIRROR

The mirror grins
I walk out from its broken mouth
It grins again
I falter
and pause before the glass fence

The mirror weeps
I walk out from its icy tears
The tears dry up
and I am caught in between
I understand at last
that no mirror can bear fracture
but if it insists on not breaking
(As it does)
So shall I by not walking through

镜子

镜子笑了
我从它破裂的嘴里走出
它第二次又笑了
我趑趄不前
我在玻璃栅栏前停住

镜子哭了
我从它冰冷的眼泪中走出
走了一半泪就干了
我从干了的梦里走出
我终于明白
没有一面镜子经得起摔
可它坚持不破
它不破
我也就赖着不出来

BIRDS WORDS

They open their mouths

and give the world a smiling Schubert

It seems spring is responsible

for their good mood

All the flowers

squint, pout, and prick up their ears

on hearing the snow's impudent laughter

deep in the mountains, after a rebirth

Their heartfelt songs

Intoxicate, and shake

the new buds on the willow tree

All at once they go mute

alarmed at having seen

a caterpillar make its way

sedulously

into the heart of a flower

鸟语

一张嘴
便是笑容满面的舒伯特
显然，它们有了好心情
春是理由之一
所有的花朵
都眯着眼，翘着唇，竖起耳朵
倾听深山里
雪的
脱胎换骨后放肆的笑声
总之，它们开怀地唱了
把柳枝上的新绿
醉得
摇摇晃晃

突然它们全都哑了
怔怔地望着
一只毛毛虫
缓缓地爬进了花蕊

DEATH IN THE STONE CELL

1

By chance I raised my eyes toward the neighboring corridor,
I was stunned
At dawn, that man rebelled against death with his naked body
Allowed a black tributary to roar through his veins
I was stunned, my eyes swept over the stone wall
Gouging out two channels of blood on its surface

My face spreads like a tree, a tree grown in fire
All is still, behind eyelids only the pupils move
Move in a direction most people fear to mention
And I am a bitter pear tree, cut down
On my annual rings you can still hear wind and cicada

石室之死亡

一

只偶然昂首向邻居的甬道，我便怔住
在清晨，那人以裸体去背叛死
任一条黑色支流咆哮横过他的脉管
我便怔住，我以目光扫过那座石壁
上面即凿成两道血槽

我的面容展开如一株树，树在火中成长
一切静止，唯眸子在眼睑后面移动
移向许多人都怕谈及的方向
而我确是那株被锯断的苦梨
在年轮上，你仍可听清楚风声，蝉声

2

In reply to those who knock, the brass ring answers with the glories of
     the past
My brothers will come and drink and anxiety filling my brow
Their thirst and hunger like an indoor plant
When I squint, metallic sounds
Clang inside the walls, fall on the guests' dishes

Afterwards it's an afternoon of debate
all sorts of filth is revealed
Languages are just a pile of dirty laundry
They are like wounded beasts unable to find permanent shelter
If the tree's silhouette were sundered by the sun
Its height would make me feel as solemn as when I face the setting sun

3

Like tree roots subject to nobody's will
But still struggling to lift the darkness filling the mountains
Like wild strawberries indifferent to eugenics
Allowing their offspring to wander over the marsh
Scolded by servants, I finished many dawns

Oh, you grower of grapes on the rock, the sun leans over you
When I reach to deeper strata, clutching lively root hairs
Then I'll gladly drown in your blood
To be the skin on your fruit, the bark on your stems
I'm humble as the number on a condemned man's back

二

凡是敲门的，铜环仍应以昔日的煊耀
弟兄们俱将来到，俱将共饮我满额的急躁
他们的饥渴犹如室内一盆素花
当我微微启开双眼，便有金属声
叮当自壁间，坠落在客人们的餐盘上

其后就是一个下午的激辩，诸般不洁的显示
语言只是一堆未曾洗涤的衣裳
遂被伤害，他们如一群寻不到恒久居处的兽
设使树的侧影被阳光劈开
其高度便予我以面临日暮时的冷肃

三

宛如树根之不依靠谁的旨意
而奋力托起满山的深沉
宛如野生草莓不讲究优生的婚媾
让子女们走遍了沼泽
我乃在奴仆的呵责下完成了许多早晨

在岩石上种植葡萄的人啦，太阳俯首向你
当我的臂伸向内层，紧握跃动的根须
我就如此乐意在你的血中溺死
为你果实的表皮，为你茎干的服饰
我卑微亦如死囚背上的号码

Joy, it always resembles someone's name

A weight concealed within, at the edge of the unknown

Grain creates a crisis in the embryo of an illicit marriage

They say the demeanor of my tongue

Is enough to cause insanity in all the piranhas of the Amazon

Thus all change is predictable

Everyone can find the fingerprint of a name after it is teased

Everyone has a few customs like receding footsteps

If you just want to laugh but cannot simply laugh

Then I'll kill all songs, including the joy

Translated by John Balcom

四

喜悦，总像某一个人的名字
重量隐伏其间，在不可触知的边缘
谷物们在私婚的胚胎中制造危机
他们说，我那以舌头舐尝的姿态
便足以使亚马逊河所有的红鱼如痴如魅

于是每种变化都可预测
都可找出一个名字被戏弄后的指痕
都有一些习俗如步声隐去
倘若你只想笑而笑得并不单纯
我便把所有的歌曲杀死，连喜悦在内

BEYOND SMOKE

Call your name in the surge; your name is
Already beyond a thousand sails.

Tides come, tides go.
Left shoe's print only afternoon,
Right shoe's print already evening.
The month June is at heart a very sentimental book.
The ending is so sadly beautiful
— Setting sun sinks westward.

I still gaze
At a patch of pure white in your eyes.
I kneel toward you toward yesterday toward a cloud-bud
        beautiful the whole afternoon.
Sea, why lit up among other lamps
Just this one of fumes of frenzy?

What else can we grasp?
That which has been called snow, your eyes,
Is now called
Smoke.

August 10, 1956

烟之外

在涛声中呼唤你的名字而你的名字
已在千帆之外

潮来潮去
左边的鞋印才下午
右边的鞋印已黄昏了
六月原是一本很感伤的书
结局如此之凄美
——落日西沉

你依然凝视
你眼中展示的一片纯白
我跪向你向昨日向那朵美了整个下午的云
海哟，为何在众灯之中
独点亮那一盏茫然

还能抓住甚么呢?
你那曾被称为雪的眸子
现有人叫做
烟

一九五六·八·十

BEYOND ASHES

You were yourself
So pure as to need no name
The flowers of death blossom under the soberest gaze
Thus we kneel to
The time of becoming ashes

And blushing we are nothing
Lying in a pocket like a forged coin

You are the embryo of fire, growing in self-combustion
No matter who provokes you with a pomegranate's hauteur
You angrily raise your arms violently against the sweat
You are that half-consumed candle of legend
The other half is beyond ashes

August 20, 1965

灰烬之外

你曾是自己
洁白得不需要任何名字
死之花，在最清醒的目光中开放
我们因而跪下
向即将成灰的那个时辰

而我们甚么也不是，红着脸
躲在裤袋里如一枚赝币

你是火的胎儿，在自燃中成长
无论谁以一拳石榴的傲慢招惹你
便愤然举臂，暴力逆汗水而上
你是传说中的那半截蜡烛
另一半在灰烬之外

一九六五·八·二十

WOUNDS OF TIME

1

How pale the moonlight's flesh
But the skin of my time slowly turns black
Peels away layer by layer
In the wind

2

Behind the door hangs a prewar raincoat
A discharge order in the pocket
Night-blooming cereus on the balcony
Blossoms in vain one whole night
Wounds of time continue to fester
It is so serious
That it cannot be cured even by chanting some lines of the Dharani
    mantra

3

Some say
That hair has only two colors
If not black then white
What then the tomb grass, green then yellow?

时间之伤

一

月光的肌肉何其苍白
而我时间的皮肤逐渐变黑
在风中
一层层脱落

二

门后挂着一袭战前的雨衣
口袋里装着一封退伍令
阳台上的昙花
白白地开了一夜
时间之伤在继续发炎
其严重性
决非念两句大悲咒所能化解的

三

又有人说啦
头发只有两种颜色
非黑即白
而青了又黄了的墓草呢?

4

As to our kites
They were snatched away by the sky
None have returned in one piece
The string is all that remains in our hands
Broken yet unbroken

5

As long as our bodies can feel pain
It serves to prove we have matured with time
The soil is warmed by the sleeping roots
The wind blows
One by one the bean pods burst

6

At times I vent my anger before the mirror
If only the city lights are all extinguished
Then never again to find my face
With my fist I shatter the glass
Blood oozes out

四

至于我们的风筝
被天空抓了去
就没有一只完整地回来过
手中只剩下那根绳子
犹断未断

五

只要周身感到痛
就足以证明我们已在时间里成熟
根须把泥土睡暖了
风吹过
豆荚开始一一爆裂

六

有时又不免对镜子发脾气
只要
全城的灯火一熄
就再也找不到自己的脸
一拳把玻璃击碎
有血水渗出

7

On the boulevards that year we sang march songs
Head high up, proudly entering history
We were stirred to the quick
Like water
Dripping on a red-hot iron
The names on our yellow khaki uniforms
Louder than a rifle's sharp report

But today, hearing a bugle from the barracks nearby
I suddenly rose, straightened my clothes
Then sat down again, dejected
Softly keeping time with the beat

8

Reminiscing of the old days
When we fought with our backs to the wall
…
Twilight falls all around
Horses galloping away
A glimpse of an old general's white head
Slowly
Lifting up
From the dust

七

那年我们在大街上唱着进行曲
昂昂然穿过历史
我们热得好快
如水
滴在烧红的铁板上
黄卡叽制服上的名字
比枪声更响
而今，听到隔壁军营的号声
我忽地振衣而起
又颓然坐了下去
且轻轻打着拍子

八

想当年
背水一战
……
暮色四起
马群腾空而去
隐见一位老将军的白头
从沙尘中
徐徐
仰起

9

Wading along through the water

Our bodies were formed of foam

Abruptly raising our heads

Twilight sun, beautiful as distant death

On the water's surface

Reflection of a giant bird of prey

In a flash disappearing

Can we swim the sea within ourselves?

10

In the end I took out all the wine sets

Yet it did not help

Using what little wine remained

I secretly jotted down a line in my palm

It congealed into a cube of ice

In my body was severe winter

The fire is dying, never can my bones be taken to burn

April 2, 1979

九

涉水而行
我们的身子由泡沫拼成
猛抬头
夕阳美如远方之死

水面上
一只巨鹰的倒影
一闪而没
我们能泅过自己的内海吗?

十

最后把所有的酒器搬出来
也无补于事
用残酒
在掌心暗自写下的那句话
乍然结成冰块
体内正值严冬

炉火将熄，总不能再把我的骨骼拿去烧吧

一九七九·四·二

WALKING TOWARD WANG WEI

A host of sleepy mountain birds

Rise up, startled

By the rustling moon

You made from folding writing paper.

Leaves, frightened, break up in an uproar.

Empty mountain—

Quiet, at ease, no human footfalls.

Here, only you, petting the wet moss on the stream rock.

O! Already so old!

A whole valley of spring flowers

Wither in due course.

The 10th year in T'ien-pao?* the 12th? the 15th?

Born, dead, or at leisur

All easy-going like the sunflower planted in the backyard.

And when afternoon comes

A stretch of mist spreads inside and outside your body

Leaving only the wet inkstone

Still brimming with a black stir.

With a cane, thus, you walk, strolling lazily

Toward the stream's source three miles away,

走向王维

一群瞌睡的山鸟
被你
用稿纸折成的月亮
窸窸窣窣惊起
扑翅的声音
吓得所有的树叶一哄而散
空山
阒无人迹
只有你，手抚涧边石头上的湿苔
啊！都这么老了
满谷的春花
依时而萎
天宝十年？十二年？十五年？
生得，死得，闲得
自在得如后院里手植的那株露葵
而一到下午
体内体外都是一片苍茫
唯有未干的砚池
仍蓄满了黑色的嚣骚
于是，懒懒地，策杖而行
向三里外的水穷处踱去

Stand there, with face up, to view mountains

And clouds, mists after mists,

Thin out from your bleak cold forehead.

Suddenly, you remember a beautiful line of poetry

But even before you straighten out your dishevelled hair, it has

already escaped you.

A few days ago, you were asked:

Which of your poems is the most Zen-like?

You effortlessly answered:

The third line from "Continuous Rains over Wang River Villa":

Mist over mist across water-paddies a white egret flies

After which, a whole robe of lucerne flowers

Rustled down the stone-steps.

Autumn, as it thinned,

Followed the somewhat lukewarm sunset

And disappeared into your desolate mountain retreat.

In days of heavy mountain rains:

Proofread

伫立，仰面看山
看云，暖暖辍辍地
从你荒凉的额上淡然散去
这时乍然想到一句好诗
刚整好吹乱的苍发又给忘了
前些日子，有人问起：
你哪首诗最有禅机？
你闲闲答曰：
不就是从"积雨辋川庄作"第三句中
漠漠飞去的
那只白鹭
语毕，一衣襟的紫苜蓿
沿着石阶一路籁籁抖落
秋，便瘦瘦地
随着犹温的夕阳
闪身进入了你萧索的山庄
山雨滂沱的日子
校书

Sit in meditation

Or drink from Chuangtsu's "Autumn Floods"

Or, across the rain-windows,

View wild smoke making a hairdo over the South Hill

Or, occasionally, with muffled anger,

Remember those things done against your will

All because of An Lu-shan.

Thus, trivially on trivial matters, for a whole day,

You stood, or sat, or threw down your brush and rose

And went toward the sunset at the ferry

Poled over to the other bank

By the boatman.

The fallen leaves lay in the courtyard: quiet, a whole night.

You got up in the morning

With hands behind, you sauntered to the Chungnan Ranges

And suddenly saw in the stream that

You had become so thin, thin like a green bamboo

Wavering, every joint

Unbending, every joint

When the wind rose.

I walk toward you, Wang Wei,

Walk into the emptiness prescribed for me in the last joint.

October 5, 1989

* T'ien-pao, under Emperor Hsuan Tsung of the T'ang Dynasty, ranges from 742 to
756.

坐禅
饮一点点庄子的秋水
或隔着雨窗
看野烟在为南山结着发辫
偶尔，悻悻然
回想当年为安禄山所执的
种种不甘
一天便这般琐琐碎碎地
或立，或坐，或掷笔而起
及至渡头的落日
被船夫
一篙子送到对岸
院子的落叶一宿无话
晨起
负手踽踱于终南山下
突然在溪水中
看到自己瘦成了一株青竹
风吹来
节节都在摇晃
节节都在坚持

我走向你
进入你最后一节为我预留的空白

一九八九·十·五

SONG OF THE CRICKET

Someone once said, "Overseas, I heard a cricket sing, and thought it was the one I heard when I was in the countryside of Szechuan."

Carrying from the courtyard

To the corner of the wall:

Jit, jut…Jit, jut.

Out of the stone crevice

Suddenly jumping

To a pillow under the white hairs,

Jut, jut.

Pushed from yesterday's drifting

To this day's corner of the world,

The cricket sings

But hides its head, its legs, wings.

I grope everywhere,

High in the sky, deep in the earth.

Still it is invisible.

I even tear open my breast,

But fail to find that vibrator.

The evening rain just then stopped.

蟋蟀之歌

有人说："在海外，夜晚听到蟋蟀叫，还以为就是四川乡下听到的那一只。"

从院子里
一路唱到墙脚
唧唧
从石阶的缝里
突然又跳到
白发散落的枕边　唧唧
由昨日的天涯
被追到今日的海角
仍只闻其声，不见头，脚，翅翼
探首四方八面搜索
碧落无踪
黄泉无影
裂开胸腔也找不到那具发音器
夜雨骤歇

The moon outside the window

Delivers the axe sound of a woodcutter

The stars are seething,

And the cricket's song bubbling

Like a stream.

My childhood drifts from upstream,

But tonight I am not in Ch'en-tu,

And my snores do not mean nostalgia.

Unceasing is the cricket song in my ears,

A thousand-threaded tune;

I have forgotten the year, the month, the evening,

Which city or town,

In which bus depot I have heard this song.

Jut, jut...Jit, jut.

Tonight, however, more shocking.

The cricket's cry

Meanders like River Chai-ling by my pillow,

Deep in night,

With no boat to hire;

I can only swim, follow the tides

Where the waves of the Three Gorges are sky-high

And monkeys shriek by the river bank,

And fish,

Only hot spicy bean fish lie in a green porcelain platter.

窗外有月
月光传下伐木的叮当
此时群星如沸
唧唧如泡沫，如一条小河
童年遥遥从上流漂来
今夜不在成都
鼾声难成乡愁
而耳边唧唧不绝
不绝如一首千丝万缕的歌
记不清哪年哪月哪晚
在哪个城市，哪个乡间
哪个小站听过
唧唧复唧唧
今晚唱得格外惊心

那鸣叫
如嘉陵江蜿蜒于我的枕边
深夜无处雇舟
只好溯流而洄
三峡的浪在天上
猿啸在两岸
鱼
豆瓣鱼在青瓷盘中

Jut, jut.

Which cricket is really singing?

The Cantonese one sings the loneliest,

The Szechuan the saddest,

And the Peking cricket, the noisiest.

But the Hunan cricket sings.

With the taste of spicy heat.

Yet, what finally woke me

Was that one in lane at San-chang Li,

The softest, the dearest

Singing of all.

July 4, 1985

唧唧
究竟是哪一只在叫？
广东的那只其声苍凉
四川的那只其声悲伤
北平的那只其声聒噪
湖南的那只叫起来带有一股辣味
而最后——
我被吵醒的
仍是三张犁巷子里
那声最轻最亲的
唧唧

一九八五·七·四

THE EARTHWORM POLLING
EARTHS GRIEVANCE
SECTION BY SECTION

Earth—

Worm glutted itself on the soil's melancholy

Arteries full of blood so cold,

when will it boil?

Section by section, veins bulging

    forcefully approaching

    a spiralling dream of darkness, by inches

    by poles, penetrating the rock-hard ages

Measured the plains, and measuring

The Grand Canyon, stirring up the sky

Overturning the earth, and thereafter it raises

Its uninspired

Head

Choked by sadness, unfeelingly

Sulking in emotion, understated and earthy

蚯蚓一节节丈量大地的悲情（隐题诗）

蚯
蚓饱食泥土的忧郁
一腔冷血何时才能沸腾？
节节青筋暴露
　　　节节逼进向一个蜿蜒的黑梦，一寸一
　　　丈地穿透坚如岩石的时间
量过了大草原，再量
大峡谷，天翻
地覆之后它仰起黯然
的头
悲怆，淡淡的
情感，土土的

CRAB-CLAW FLOWERS

Perhaps you may not grieve over this.

Crab-claw flowers explode one by one along
the ceramic rim, and, in an instant of deep silence, all turn back
their heads.

Hand gestures at the window, a kind of deep-red depression
Caught in the net of confused green tendons
You say: Go naked!
Immediately, body fragrance brims over
One petal
Into
Another petal.

Crab-claw flowers
Stretch
And conquer the entire city of your forehead.

At the center of a most beautiful moment you say: Ouch!
Immediately, branches, leaves unfurl, water in the stalk rises to
the ear.
You are stunned.
Only when flowers split and burst like a wound
Are you able to recognize yourself.

蟹爪花

或许你并不因此而就悲哀吧
蟹爪花沿着瓦盆四周一一爆燃
且在静寂中一齐回过头来
你打着手势在窗口，在深红的绝望里
在青色筋络的纠结中你开始说：裸
便有体香溢出
一瓣
吐
再一瓣

蟹爪花
横着
占有你额上全部的天空

在最美的时刻你开始说：痛
枝叶舒放，茎中水声盈耳
你顿然怔住
在花朵绽裂一如伤口的时刻
你才辨识自己

MAILING A PAIR OF SHOES

From one-thousand miles away

I've mailed you a pair of cotton shoes

A letter

With no words

Containing more than forty years of things to say

That were only thought but never said

One sentence after another

Closely stitched into the soles

What I have to say I've kept hidden for so long

Some of it hidden beside the well

Some of it hidden in the kitchen

Some of it hidden beneath my pillow

Some of it hidden in the flickering lamp at midnight

Some of it has been dried by the wind

Some of it has grown moldy

Some of it has lost its teeth

Some of it has sprouted moss

寄鞋

间关千里
寄给你一双布鞋
一封
无字的信
积了四十多年的话
想说无从说
只好一句句
密密缝在鞋底

这些话我偷偷藏了很久
有几句藏在井边
有几句藏在厨房
有几句藏在枕头下
有几句藏在午夜明灭不定的灯火里
有的风干了
有的生霉了
有的掉了牙齿
有的长出了青苔

Now I gather it all together

And closely stitch it into the soles

The shoes may perhaps be too small

I measured them with my heart, with our childhood

With dreams deep in the night

Whether they fit or not is another matter

Keep them by all means

Even if they wear out

Forty years of thought

Forty years of lonliness

Are all stitched into the soles

Note: My friend Chang To-wu and Miss Ch'en Lian-tzu were engaged when very Young, but because of the war they parted and were separated by a great distance, unable to communicate with one another for more than forty years. a friend managed to deliver a pair of cotton shoes sewn and sent by Miss Ch'en. T'o-wu received them as if receiving a wordless letter full of words from home. He wept and sighed, unable to stop. Today T'o-wu and Miss Ch'en are both grown old, but their love is without end. This poem is written from the point of view of Miss Ch'en, therefore the language has been kept simple and clear.

现在——收集起来
密密缝在鞋底
鞋子也许嫌小一些
我是以心裁量，以童年
以五更的梦裁量
合不合脚是另一回事
请千万别弃之
若敝屣
四十多年的思念
四十多年的孤寂
全部缝在鞋底

后记：好友张拓芜与表妹沈莲子自小订婚，因战乱在家乡分手后，天涯海角，不相问闻已逾四十余年，近透过海外友人，突接获表妹寄来亲手缝制的布鞋一双，拓芜捧着这双鞋，如捧一对无字而千言万语尽在其中的家书，不禁涕泪纵横，唏嘘不已。现拓芜与表妹均已老去，但情之为物，却是生生世世难以熄灭。本诗乃假借沈莲子的语气写成，故用辞力求浅白。

AT LENIN'S TOMB

The guards no longer use guns

To support the dead man's meditative jaw.

The mouth occasionally trembles as if

To recite a long-winded moldy lecture.

Grief keeps hiding behind

Piled-up revolutionary texts

And long fires of tobacco and

Potato buyers.

Losing no time, I raise my camera

To snap the feeling of snow at the grave

And when developed it turns out to be

A flock of doves about to fly.

列宁墓前
—— （苏联诗抄之二）

卫兵不再用枪
支持死者沉思的下颚
嘴巴偶而颤动犹之
在背诵那篇冗长而带点霉味的讲词
悲怆，总是藏在
厚厚的革命论著中，以及
买烟草与马铃薯的
长长的队伍中
我用照相机
提前将墓前的雪意拍下
冲洗出来的竟是
一群振翅欲飞的白鸽

MAYAKOVSKY'S STATUE AND BIRD SHIT

1

The admirer

Wishes he could raise himself

As high as Mayakovsky's statue

But the bird shit is

Even higher

2

He once stuck his head in a blast furnace

Saying

A good poem can take a hot fire

But how could white bird shit

Go together with red history?

Since he was cast into a statue

His eyes have been green with agony.

马雅可夫斯基铜像与鸟粪
——（苏联诗抄之三）

其一

仰望者
总想把自己也提升到
马雅可夫斯基的铜像那么高
而鸟粪
比铜像更高

其二

他一度把头颅塞进炼铜炉
说是
好诗不怕火烧
可是鸟粪的白
又如何与历史的红搭配？
铸成铜像后
便苦恼得两眼发绿

THE RHETORIC OF DEATH

Gunshots

Spit out the tart smell of mustard.

My skull explodes:

In the trees,

It ripens into pomegranate.

In the sea,

It congeals into salt.

Only the blood formula remains unchanged

Sprinkled about

In the reddest hour.

This is the language of fire, wine, flowers, an exquisite

burial urn—

    all the rhetoric of death.

I was murdered

And created, a new form.

死亡的修辞学

枪声
吐出芥末的味道

我的头壳炸裂在树中
即结成石榴
在海中
即结成盐
唯有血的方程式未变
在最红的时刻
洒落

这是火的语言，酒，鲜花，精致的骨灰瓮，俱是死亡的修辞学

我被害
我被创造为一新的形式

UNMAILED LETTER

One night
Someone seemed to knock on my door

What were the fallen leaves in the yard clamoring about?
I raked them all into a large clear plastic bag
Autumn wriggled there among them

Carrying a sprig of sagebrush in its break
A robin flew passed my window
Only then did I realize that you long for the loneliness of dust
A finished letter need not be mailed
Because I just heard a skeleton
Squashed to pieces deep in the mountains

未寄

某夜
好像有人叩门

院子的落叶何事喧哗
我把它们全部扫进了
一只透明的塑料口袋
秋，在袋中蠕蠕而动

一只知更鸟衔着一匹艾草
打从窗口飞过
这时才知道你是多么向往灰尘的寂寞
写好的信也不必寄了
因为我刚听到
深山中一堆骸骨轰然碎裂的声音

SHARING A DRINK WITH LI HO*

Stones shatter

Heaven is startled

Abruptly autumn rain stops, freezing in mid-air

This moment, beyond the window I suddenly see

A traveller arrive from Ch'ang-an riding on a donkey

On his back is a cloth sack of

Horrifying images

Not yet arrive and hail-like lines of poetry

Already fall heavily with cold rain

Through the window I again hear

The astronomers His and Ho tapping on the sun

Oh, such a thin, thin scholar

So thin

Like an exquisite weasel-hair writing brush

Your large blue gown flows in the wind

Welling into a thousand waves

与李贺共饮

石破
天惊
秋雨吓得骤然凝在半空
这时，我乍见窗外
有客骑驴自长安来
背了一布袋的
骇人的意象
人未至，冰雹般的诗句
已挟冷雨而降
我隔着玻璃再一次听到
羲和敲日的叮当声
哦！好瘦好瘦的一位书生
瘦得
犹如一枝精致的狼毫
你那宽大的蓝布衫，随风
涌起千顷波涛

Chewing five-spice lima beans as if

Chewing four line poems

In your impassioned eyes

Is a pot of newly brewed Hua Tiao Wine

From T'ang to Sung to Yuan to Ming and to Ch'ing

At last it is poured into

This small wine cup of mine

I sample it by taking your most satisfying poem

And seal it in a wine urn

Shake it up, then watch as the cloud-mist arises

Language dance drunkenly, rythmes conflict chaotically

The bottle breaks, your flesh shatters into pieces

On a vast plain the screeching of ghosts

Is mysteriously heard

The howling of wolves carries over thousand of miles

嚼五香蚕豆似的
嚼着绝句。绝句。绝句。
你激情的眼中
温有一壶新酿的花雕
自唐而宋而元而明而清
最后注入
我这小小的酒杯
我试着把你最得意的一首七绝
塞进一只酒瓮中
摇一摇，便见云雾腾升
语字醉舞而平仄乱撞
瓮破，你的肌肤碎裂成片
旷野上，隐闻
鬼哭啾啾
狼嗥千里

Come, please sit down, I wish to share a drink with you

On this the blackest night in history

You and I are obviously not from among the run of the mill

How can we be troubled at not being included in the "Three
Hundred Poems of the T'ang Dynasty"

Of what use are the nine grades of offical rank?

They're not worth bothering about

Then, you were also deeply drunk

Vomiting poems on the jade steps at a palatial door

Drink, drink

Tonight's moon probably will not shine

For this our once in an aeon meeting

I wish to take advantage of the blackness to write an ambiguous
poems

Incomprehensible, then let them not understand

Not understand

Why after reading we gaze at one another and burst into laughter

*Li Ho, a famous poet in the T'ang Dynasty, 790-816

来来请坐，我要与你共饮
这历史中最黑的一夜
你我显非等闲人物
岂能因不入唐诗三百首而相对发愁
从九品奉礼郎是个甚么官？
这都不必去管它
当年你还不是在大醉后
把诗句呕吐在豪门的玉阶上
喝酒呀喝酒

今晚的月，大概不会为我们
这千古一聚而亮了
我要趁黑为你写一首晦涩的诗
不懂就让他们去不懂
不懂
为何我们读后相视大笑

GOLDEN DRAGON TEMPLE

The evening bell
Is a small trail travellers take descending the mountain
Ferns
Along steps of white stone
Chewed up, down the path

If this place were covered with snow…

But all that's seen rise
Is a single startled rise of cicada
Lighting the lanterns
All over the mountain
One by one

金龙禅寺

晚钟
是游客下山的小路
羊齿植物
沿着白色的石阶
一路嚼了下去

如果此处降雪

而只见
一只惊起的灰蝉
把山中的灯火
一盏盏的
点燃

PEELING PEARS AT MIDNIGHT

Chilly and thirsty,

Silent, I stare

At a Korean pear

On a midnight tea-stand.

That is really

An icy

Bronzed-colored

Pear.

Sit in half, it has

Deep in its chest,

Such a deep, deep well.

Trembling with my thumb and index finger,

I pick up a sliver of pear.

White innocence.

My knife drops.

I bend down to find

Oh! All over the floor

Peeling of my bronze-colored skin.

午夜削梨
——（汉城诗抄之七）

冷而且渴
我静静地望着
午夜的茶几上
一只韩国梨

那确是一只
触手冰凉的
闪着黄铜肤色的
梨
一刀剖开
它胸中
竟然藏有
一口好深好深的井

战栗着
拇指与食指轻轻捻起
一小片梨肉

白色无罪
刀子跌落
我弯下身去找
啊！满地都是
我那黄铜色的皮肤

METAPHYSICAL GAME

The dice is grasped then cast

Spinning

A frightful whirlpool

The Gods are silent

Five fingers suddenly open

Begin to sweat

Heaven and earth

Black and yellow

In a bowl

    dripping

        running

            spinning

From a black hole in the milky way

Far away comes a startled cry

As stars lose their footing and fall

形而上的游戏

一把骰子掷下去
飞旋着
一个惊怖的漩涡
众神静默

五指骤张
开始冒汗
天地
玄黄
在碗中
滴
　　溜
　　　　溜
　　　　　地，飞旋
银河系的黑洞中
遥遥传来星群失足时的
惊呼

That concave silhouette

Rolls

Creaking noisily

Moving, is limitless vitality

All forms of existence

Going around on the wheel of transmigration

Round and round

Rolling, crawling

On a sorrowful journey

Before five fingers open

The Gods are silent

When all the temple bells ring

One after another

The universe held in the palm of a hand

Slowly shrinks into

An egg

A stone

A cube of

Rolling unknown

Impossible to foretell

Lost

Is yesterday's boundless sea

    tomorrow's mulberry orchard

or aeons of endless change observed

那凹形的侧面
滚动着
或然率叮当作响
动，是无限生机
是存在的诸多样式
是一次又一次的轮回
一次又一次
连滚带爬的
悲怆的旅程

五指未张开之前
众神静默
当所有寺院的钟声
次第响起
掌中盈握的宇宙
逐渐缩小为
一卵
一石
一方方的
滚动的未知
谁也无从预测
轮掉的
是昨日的沧海
　　　明日的桑田
抑或亿万年来看尽白云苍狗

The unpredictable variegations in the sky

Five fingers

Before opening

Are the tempest in the palm of a hand

The struggle between life and death

Or just a metaphysical game

A poorly edited book, filled with errors

Neither to be believed

Nor denied

Released

It falls

Spinning

An enchanting whirl pool

Soft ward and hard ward

Analysis and reasoning

I Ching and astrology

All useless for knowing

苍狗白云的天空
五指
未张开之前
是掌底大风暴
是生死大对决
或只是一场形而上的游戏
一本错字连篇的经书
信也不是
不信也不是

撒手
掷下去了
飞旋者
一个诱人深入的漩涡
软体以及硬体
分析以及推理
易经以及紫微斗数
皆无助于预知

How our lives are arranged

Where we will board ship

Where we will land

More useless yet for determining

Are those deep red spots

Scars or birth marks?

Randomly cast

They spin and run

Rolling back to the very beginning

Universe

Primeval chaos

In a veil of mist

The silent Gods

Look down at

A frightful whirlpool

我们一生将如何被安排——
安排于何处登舟
何处上岸
更无从辨识
那深红的点子
是伤疤？抑或胎记？
随便一掷
便滴溜溜地
滚回了太初
宇宙
洪洪荒荒
在烟雾迷濛中
众神静默
俯视着
一个惊怖的漩涡

图书在版编目（CIP）数据

洛夫诗歌英译选 / 杨四平主编. -- 上海：上海文
化出版社, 2023.3
（当代汉诗英译丛书）
ISBN 978-7-5535-2692-8

Ⅰ.①洛… Ⅱ.①杨… Ⅲ.①诗集—中国—当代—汉、英 Ⅳ.
①I227

中国国家版本馆CIP数据核字(2023)第027519号

出　版　人：姜逸青
责任编辑：黄慧鸣　张　彦
装帧设计：王　伟

书　　名：洛夫诗歌英译选
主　　编：杨四平
出　　版：上海世纪出版集团　上海文化出版社
地　　址：上海市闵行区号景路159弄A座3楼　201101
发　　行：上海文艺出版社发行中心
　　　　　上海市闵行区号景路159弄A座2楼　201101　www.ewen.co
印　　刷：苏州市越洋印刷有限公司
开　　本：889×1194　1/32
印　　张：4.375
印　　次：2023年6月第一版　2023年6月第一次印刷
书　　号：ISBN 978-7-5535-2692-8/I.1037
定　　价：45.00元
告 读 者：如发现本书有质量问题请与印刷厂质量科联系　T：0512-68180628